Books by Sid Fleischman

Mr. Mysterious and Company
By the Great Horn Spoon!
The Ghost in the Noonday Sun
Chancy and the Grand Rascal
Longbeard the Wizard
Jingo Django
The Wooden Cat Man
The Ghost on Saturday Night
Mr. Mysterious's Secrets of Magic
McBroom Tells a Lie
Me and the Man on the Moon-Eyed Horse
McBroom and the Beanstalk
Humbug Mountain
The Hey Hey Man
McBroom and the Great Race
McBroom's Ghost
McBroom Tells the Truth
McBroom the Rainmaker
McBroom and the Big Wind
McBroom's Zoo
McBroom's Ear

McBROOM'S
Ear

McBROOM's
Ear

SID FLEISCHMAN

Illustrated by Walter Lorraine

An Atlantic Monthly Press Book
Little, Brown and Company
BOSTON   TORONTO

TEXT COPYRIGHT © 1969 BY SID FLEISCHMAN

ILLUSTRATIONS COPYRIGHT © 1982 BY WALTER LORRAINE

Library of Congress Cataloging in Publication Data

Fleischman, Sid, 1920–
  McBroom's ear.

  "An Atlantic Monthly Press book."
  Summary: The war is on when the grasshoppers
attack Josh McBroom's fabulous one-acre farm and
prize ear of corn.
  [1. Humorous stories. 2. Farm life—Fiction]
I. Lorraine, Walter H., ill. II. Title.
PZ7.F5992Maf 1982   [Fic]   81–15636
ISBN 0–316–28539–0   AACR2
ISBN 0–316–28540–4 (pbk.)

ATLANTIC-LITTLE, BROWN BOOKS
ARE PUBLISHED BY
LITTLE, BROWN AND COMPANY
IN ASSOCIATION WITH
THE ATLANTIC MONTHLY PRESS

AHS

*Published simultaneously in Canada
by Little, Brown & Company (Canada) Limited*

PRINTED IN THE UNITED STATES OF AMERICA

For Melanie

GRASSHOPPERS—yes, they did get wind of our wonderful one-acre farm. The long-legged, saw-legged, hop-legged rascals ate us out of house and home.

You know how grasshoppers are. They'd as soon

1

spit tobacco juice as look at you. And they're terribly hungry creatures. I guess there's nothing that can eat more in less time than a swarm of grasshoppers. Green things, especially, make their mouths water.

I don't intend to talk about it with a hee and a haw. Mercy, no! If you know me—Josh McBroom—you know I'd as soon live in a tree as tamper with the truth.

I'd best start with the weather. Summer was just waking up, but the days weren't near warm enough yet for grasshoppers. The young'uns were helping me to dig a water well. They talked of growing one thing and another to enter in the County Fair.

I guess you've heard how amazing rich our farm is. Anything will grow in it—quick. Seeds burst in the ground and crops shoot right up before your eyes. Why, just yesterday our oldest boy dropped a five-cent piece and before he could find it that nickel had grown to a quarter.

Early one morning a skinny, tangle-haired stranger came ambling along the road. My, he was tall! I do believe if his hat fell off it would take a day or two to reach the ground.

"Howdy, sir," he said. "I'm Slim-Face John from here, there, and other places. I'll paint your barn cheap."

That man was not only tall, skinny, and tangle-haired, he was nearsighted. "We don't own a barn," I said.

He squinted and laughed. "In that case," he said, "I'll paint it free."

"Done." I smiled.

He painted that no-barn in less than a second, with time left over. He appeared to be hungry, so my dear wife, Melissa, gave him a hearty break- fast and he went ambling away. "I'll be back." He waved.

The young'uns and I kept digging that well. My, it was hard work. They'd lower a bucket, I'd fill it with earth, and they'd haul it up like a tug-of-war. All eleven of them.

The days grew longer and hotter. Flies began to drop out of the air with sunstroke.

But it still wasn't grasshopper weather.

"Will*jill*hester*chester*peter*polly*tim*tom*mary-*larry*andlittle*clarinda*!" I had to shout from the bottom of the well. "Work to do! Haul up the bucket!"

"Aw, Pa," Chester complained from the tree

house. "I'm fixin' to grow a prize watermelon for the Fair. A fifty-pounder."

"I think I'll grow a pumpkin," Polly said.

"Well, I'm growing impatient!" I said. "Haul up the bucket, my lambs, and dump it. County Fair's still a week off."

The next day was a real sizzler. At high noon the yellow wax beans began melting on the vines. They dripped like candles.

No—it wasn't grasshopper weather yet. The leggy creatures would catch cold on a chilly day like that.

We finished the well at last, with the bucketfuls of earth standing in a big heap beside it. Along about supper time that tall, skinny, tangle-haired, nearsighted stranger was back.

"Howdy," he said. "I'm Slim-Face John from

here, there, and other places. I'll dig you a water
well cheap."

"We've got a well," I said.

"In that case," he answered, "I'll dig it free."

He stayed for supper and then went ambling
away. "I'll be back." He waved.

Another day passed. The sunball began to outdo
itself.

Hot? Why, the next morning it was so infernal
hot that a block of ice felt warm to the touch.

Mama had to boil water to cool it off. Sunflowers along the road picked up their roots and hurried under the trees for shade.

That was grasshopper weather.

Just after breakfast the first jumpers arrived. They came in twos and fours. Our farm stood green as an emerald and it was bound to catch their eye. Before long they were turning up in sixes and eights.

I must admit those first visitors surprised us

with their nice table manners. They didn't spit tobacco juice any which way. Peter set out an old coffee can and they used it for a spittoon.

By noon hop-legs were arriving by the fifties and hundreds. They nibbled our cabbage and lettuce, but it was nothing to be alarmed about. We could grow vegetables faster than they could eat them—three or four crops a day.

Along about sundown the saw-legged visitors came whirring in by the hundreds and the

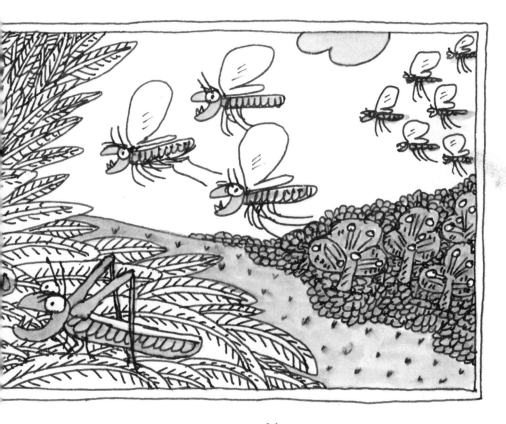

thousands. I wasn't worried. Grasshoppers are hardly worth counting in small numbers like that.

"Pa," Chester said at breakfast. "County Fair's tomorrow. Reckon it's time to set out my watermelons."

"I'm going to grow a prize tomato," Mary declared. "Big as a balloon."

"You young'uns use the patch behind the

house," I said. "I aim to plant the farm in corn."

The grasshoppers didn't get in our way. Larry and little Clarinda fed them turnip greens out of their hands. I got the field planted in no time.

My, it was fine corn-growing weather. The stalks leaped right up, dangling with ears.

Suddenly, a silvery green cloud rose off the horizon and raced toward us.

Grasshoppers!

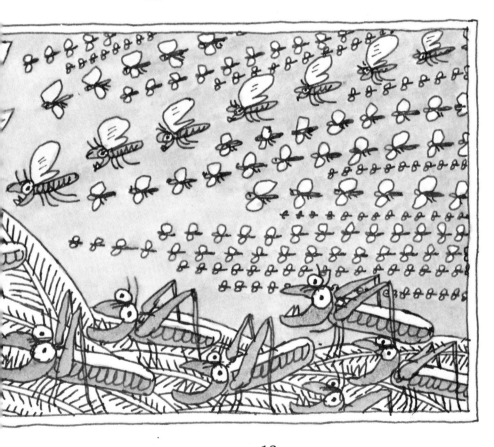

Grasshoppers by the thousands! Grasshoppers by the millions! Little did we know it was the beginning of the Great Grasshopper War—or, as it came to be called, the War of McBroom's Ear.

"Will*jill*hester*chester*peter*polly*tim*tom*mary-*larry*andlittle*clarinda*!" I shouted. "Brooms and branches! Shoo them off!"

We began yelling and running about and waving our weapons. The grasshoppers spun over our ripening cornfield. They feasted their eyes—and flew off.

"We—scared 'em away!" Tim declared.

"No," I said. "That was just the advance party. They went back for the main herd. *And here they come!*"

Acres of grasshoppers! Square miles of grasshoppers! They came streaking toward us like a great roaring thunderbolt of war.

"Brooms and branches!" I yelled.

The hungry devils tucked napkins under their chins and swooped down for the attack. Mercy! The air got so thick with hoppers you could swing a bucket once and fill it twice. They made a whirring, hopping, jumping fog. We could barely see a foot beyond our noses.

But we could hear the ravenous rascals. They

were chomping and chewing up our cornfield and spitting out the cobs. They ate that farm right down to the ground in exactly four seconds flat.

Then they rose in the air, still hungry as wolves, and waited for the next crop.

"Pa!" Chester said. "They skinned my watermelons!"

"Pa!" Mary cried. "They didn't even wait for my

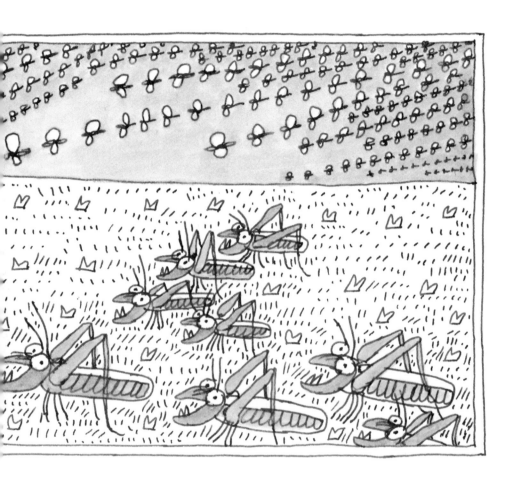

prize tomatoes to ripen. They ate them green!"

"Pa!" little Clarinda said. "What happened to your socks?"

I looked down. Glory be! Those infernal dinner guests had eaten the socks right out of my shoes — green socks. All they left were the holes in the toes.

Some of the young'uns broke into tears. "We

won't be able to grow anything for the County
Fair!"

"We're not beat yet, my lambs," I said, thinking
as hard as I could. "Those hoppers did have us
outnumbered, but not outsmarted. I'm going to
town for seed. Better clear away the corncobs."

I drove to town in our air-cooled Franklin
automobile and was back before noon with fifty

pounds of fine seed. The grasshoppers were still stretched all over the sky, waiting. The young'uns had cleared the farm, throwing the corncobs on the heap of dirt beside the well.

"Not a moment to lose," I said. "Help scatter the seed."

Before long our farm was bushed out, green as a one-acre jungle. Those hoppers smacked their lips and fought to get at it. They whirred and swarmed

and cranched and crunched—that crop disappeared as if sucked up by a tornado.

Well, you should have seen how surprised they were! That first wave of hoppers was all but breathing fire. And no wonder. They had dined on hot green peppers.

They streaked off in a hurry, looking for something to drink.

Of course, there were still tons of grasshoppers left. We kept sowing crops of hot green peppers all afternoon until there wasn't a jump-leg to be seen. We found out later they had swarmed to a lake in the next county and drunk it dry.

But they'd be back. The young'uns would have to grow their prizewinners in a hurry.

"Pa—look!" little Clarinda shouted.

She was pointing to the tall heap of dirt, littered with corncobs. Glory be! The grasshoppers had missed a lone kernel and it had taken root behind our backs. A cornstalk was growing up as big as a tree.

That dirt hill was powerful rich. The roots of that wondrous stalk were having a banquet! A single ear of corn began to form before our eyes. Big? Why, it was already fatter than a potbellied stove and still growing.

"That looks like a prizewinner to me!" I declared. "You scamps will go partners."

Jill and Hester and Polly climbed to their treehouse to keep a sharp eye out for grasshoppers. That ear of corn grew longer and fatter. It was a beauty! The stalk began to bend under its weight. And it was ripening fast.

Didn't we get busy, though! We fixed loops of rope around that ear so as to let it down easy. Will climbed up a ladder with a bucksaw and went to work. It must have taken him five minutes to saw that giant ear off the stalk.

We eased it down with the ropes. I tell you, we could hardly believe our eyes. That ear of corn was so big you couldn't see it in a single glance. You had to look twice.

"Grasshoppers!" Jill shouted from the treehouse. "Grasshoppers coming, Pa!"

"Quick," I said. "Into the house!"

It took all of us to lift that ear of corn. But it wouldn't fit through the door. And it wouldn't fit through the window.

"The well!" I shouted.

We lowered it by ropes and covered the well over

with some rusty sheets of corrugated tin. And just in time. Those hoppers had spotted our great ear from the sky and came whirring across the farm in a green blizzard. But they couldn't get at that ear of corn.

"It's safe for the night," I said.

"How will we *ever* get it past the hoppers to the Fair tomorrow?" Mary asked.

I don't have to tell you the problem gave me a
sleepless night. About four in the morning I
jumped out of bed and woke the young'uns.

"Brooms and buckets!" I said. "Follow me."

We tiptoed outside, careful not to wake the
jump-legs. We quietly raised our ear of corn from
the well and replaced the sheets of corrugated tin.
Then I filled the buckets from the shed.

"Start painting," I whispered.

The young'uns dipped their brooms and painted

that giant corn ear from end to end and all over.

At sunup the grasshoppers rose from the fields and went looking for breakfast. They headed straight for the well, banging their heads on the rusty tin. My, what a clatter! They thought our enormous big ear was still down there.

Well, it was in plain sight. Only they didn't recognize it. The husk wasn't green anymore. We had *whitewashed* it.

We lifted it to the roof of the old Franklin and

tied it down. "Everybody pile in." I smiled, start-
ing up the motor. "We're off to the Fair!"

Just then Mr. Slim-Face John came along.

"Howdy." He smiled. "I'll paint your farmhouse
cheap."

"Oh, I'd dearly like that," Mama said. "Red,
with white windowsills."

"Done," I said. "You'll find paint in the shed."
And we were off.

Well, you should have seen heads turn along the way. What *was* that thing on the roof of our car? An ear of corn? No sir! No farmer can raise corn that big. And white as chalk!

We bumped along the dirt road, following signs to the County Fair. We enjoyed the sights—barns,

and silos, and cows chewing their cuds in the shade.

"How much farther?" Polly asked.

"Ten, twelve miles," I said. "Be patient."

I noticed the prairie windmills begin to turn. A hot wind was coming up, dragging a cloud with it. We could hear the rumble of thunder.

"How much farther, Pa?" Tim asked.

"Eight, ten miles," I said. "Be patient."

But I didn't like the look of that cloud. It grew darker and heavier and came blowing our way.

"Heads in!" I called to the young'uns. "Thunder shower ahead."

We met the storm head on. It didn't amount to much, but those raindrops were almost hot enough to scald you. They bounced like sparks off the hood. A moment later the sky was blue again and the summer shower behind us.

"How much farther, Pa?" Mary asked.

"Six, eight miles," I said. "Be patient."

"Pa," Will said. He hadn't bothered to pull his head in the window and his hair was wet. "Pa, look what's happened to our corn!"

I jammed on the brakes and got out to see. Lo and behold—the husk was bright green again! The summer shower had washed off the whitewash.

I jumped back behind the wheel and off we spun. "Watch for grasshoppers," I shouted.

"I'm watching, Pa," little Clarinda answered. *"And here they come!"*

Well, it was a race. The hoppers came roaring after us in full battle formation. The old Franklin creaked and groaned and clanked, but her heart was in it. We bumped in and out of the ruts and jumped a few.

33

"They're gaining on us, Pa!"

I had the foot pedal to the floorboard. Soon we could see the flags and banners of the County Fair ahead.

But not soon enough. The first hop-legs were landing on the roof and we could hear them ripping and tearing at the husk. By the time we reached the fairgrounds we'd have nothing left but the cob.

But the old Franklin started to backfire, banging and booming something fierce. Those hop-legs jumped a mile and we made it across the fairgrounds.

I charged right into the main-exhibition building and jammed on the brakes. "Shut all the doors!" I shouted. "Grasshoppers! Grasshoppers coming!"

The doors swung shut and we could breathe easy

at last. Folks began to cluster around, their eyes rising as their jaws fell open at the wonder of our ear of corn. And I declare if the hungry rascals hadn't husked it neat as you please.

We lifted it down off the roof and put it on display. The judges came by and asked what name to enter it by.

"McBroom." I smiled. "Will*jill*hester*chester*-peter*polly*tim*tom*mary*larry*andlittle*clarinda*—McBroom!"

Well, the judges gave it first, second, third prize and honorable mention, too. But, my, it was getting overheated in there with the doors closed.

The young'uns lined up to have their picture taken for the county paper. There was one long smile reaching from Will at one end to little Clarinda at the other. The noon sun kept beating down on the roof and all of a sudden there came a loud bang.

I thought at first it was our tired old Franklin. But no. It was the young'uns' enormous, big prize-winning ear of corn—beginning to pop! The inside of that building had grown so infernal hot it was a perfect popcorn popper.

Well, it did get noisy in there! Kernels swelled and exploded like great white cannon balls. They

bounced off the roof and the walls. Pop-pop-pop.
Pop. Pop-pop-pop-pop-pop! Folks ducked and
others ran. Corn in their rows boomed away in
regular broadsides! I tell you popcorn was flying
all over the hall and piling up like a heavy
snowfall. Pop- pop-pop-pop-pop-pop-pop-pop! In no
time at all we were buried in light, fluffy popcorn.
It swelled to the roof and forced open the doors. It
overflowed the building at both ends.

There wasn't a grasshopper left in sight. All that ruckus had sent them flying. As far as I know they headed for the full moon. Must have heard it was made of green cheese. We never saw them again.

We stayed the afternoon—everyone did. Folks melted up buckets of prize butter and someone went to town for barrels of salt. There was more than enough fresh popcorn to go around. Salted and buttered, it was delicious. One piece was enough to feed an entire family.

Did I tell you I'd as soon live in a tree as tamper with the truth? Well, when we got back that night we found our farmhouse chawed and gnawed and eaten to the ground. Mr. Slim-Face John was not only tall, skinny, tangle-haired, and nearsighted. He was also color blind. Painted our house green.

Yes—it's a mite crowded living up here in the young'uns' treehouse. But those prize ribbons— they're all mighty nice to look at.